WEST CHICAGO PUBLIC LIBRARY DISTRICT

WD

3 6653 00163 9164

W9-AAE-544

West Chicago Public Library District
118 West Washington
West Chicago, IL 60185-2803
Phone # (630) 231-1552

This book
is dedicated
to my Uncle Charley,
"Chuck,"
who also had
and old blue truck.

Walter Lorraine (wr) Books

Copyright © 2006 by Peggy Perry Anderson

All rights reserved. For information about permission
to reproduce selections from this book, write to Permissions,
Houghton Mifflin Company, 215 Park Avenue South,
New York, New York 10003.

www.houghtonmifflinbooks.com

Library of Congress Cataloging-in-Publication Data
Anderson, Peggy Perry.
   Chuck's truck / by Peggy Perry Anderson.
     p. cm.
   "Walter Lorraine books."
   Summary: When too many barnyard friends climb in to go to town, Chuck's
truck breaks down, but Handyman Hugh knows just what to do.
   ISBN-13: 978-0-618-66836-6
   ISBN-10: 0-618-66836-5
[1. Trucks—Fiction. 2. Domestic animals—Fiction. 3. Stories in rhyme.] I. Title.
   PZ8.3.A5484Chu 2006
   [E]—dc22

                        2005020870

Printed in Singapore
TWP 10 9 8 7 6 5 4 3 2 1

This is Chuck.

3

This is Chuck's truck.
Chuck rides in his truck.

The duck Luck rides in the truck with Chuck.

The chicken that goes "cluck" rides in the truck with the duck Luck and Chuck.

Chuck's dogs, Nip and Tuck, climb on too.

The burro Buck jumps into the truck.

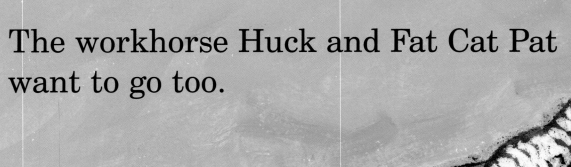

The workhorse Huck and Fat Cat Pat
want to go too.

Don't forget about
Sue and Lou!

And then they meet
the old goat Flo. And so . . .

when they
get to town . . .

the truck

BOOM!

down!

So Sue and Lou and the
goat Flo too, Nip and Tuck
and the burro Buck, Fat Cat Pat
and the workhorse Huck with

the duck Luck, the chicken that
goes "cluck," and Chuck
get a friend to tow the truck.

Chuck is sad.
The animals hope
it's not *that* bad.

They call for
help from
Handyman Hugh.

He hurries over with his whole crew.

They know exactly what to do.

Together they make the truck like new.

Here is Chuck.

And here is Chuck's truck

all ready to go to town.

This time Chuck's truck will
NOT
break down!